the Girl Who Wouldn't Brush Her Hair

by Kate Bernheimer
illustrated by Jake Parker

schwartz & wade books · new york

For Xia, my hero, and protector of creatures both large and small —K.B.

For Lucy, whose locks would make a cozy mouse house —J.P.

Text copyright © 2013 by Kate Bernheimer
Cover art and interior illustrations copyright © 2013 by Jake Parker

All rights reserved. Published in the United States by
Schwartz & Wade Books, an imprint of Random House Children's Books,
a division of Random House, Inc., New York.

Schwartz & Wade Books and the colophon are trademarks of
Random House, Inc.

Visit us on the Web! randomhouse.com/kids

Educators and librarians, for a variety of teaching tools, visit us at
RHTeachersLibrarians.com

Library of Congress Cataloging-in-Publication Data
Bernheimer, Kate.
The girl who wouldn't brush her hair / by Kate Bernheimer ;
illustrated by Jake Parker. — 1st ed.   p. cm.
Summary: A little girl refuses to brush her hair, but when a team of
mice takes up residence in her tangled locks, she faces a tough
decision—to brush or not to brush.
ISBN 978-0-375-86878-8 (trade) — ISBN 978-0-375-96878-5 (glb)
[1. Hair—Care and hygiene—Fiction. 2. Cleanliness—Fiction. 3. Mice—Fiction.]
I. Parker, Jake. ill. II. Title. III. Title: Girl who would not brush her hair.
PZ7.B45566 Gk 2013
[E]—dc23
2012006440

The text of this book is set in Filosofia.
The illustrations were rendered in pencil and colored digitally.

MANUFACTURED IN CHINA
10 9 8 7 6

First Edition

There once was a girl who wouldn't brush her hair. Her hair was wonderful—bear-brown and wavy. The girl also had a doll that looked just like her, except the doll had no hair and was only a baby. The doll's name was Baby.

After the girl's bath every evening, she'd pile a
turban upon her head and pretend she was queen.

At bedtime, she would unravel the turban and let her hair fall down in a tangled heap. No brushing. "It's just my way," she explained to the grown-ups. And then she'd lie down beside Baby and begin to dream.

This went on for a great many evenings—the hair-washing, the turban, the not-brushing, the dreams. It was wonderful, really. Until one night, the girl unwound the turban, and what was that? Oh, dear. A little mouse had taken up residence in a particularly tangled place in her hair.

Now, we all know that in books, people scream when they see a mouse, and jump on a chair. But the girl was in bed; there was no chair nearby. And besides, she'd read enough fairy tales to remember that mice always turned out to be your helpers. So she simply said, "Hello up there, mouse!" and decided to let it be.

"It's just my way," she said to the
grown-ups when they came to kiss her
good night and saw the mouse making a
cozy bed on top of her head.

The next morning, the girl awoke to
find that another mouse had moved in—
a bigger one carrying a suitcase full of fairy-
tale books. And there, by the foot of the bed,
a couple of tiny mice with rucksacks were
gazing longingly in her hair's very direction.

That day, the girl, the doll, and all the mice went to school.
It wasn't long before word got around the mouse-world that there
was a very nice home atop a girl's head, and more mice joined them.

The schoolchildren marveled at this new development. They too stopped brushing their hair, in hope of starting their own little mouse menageries. How wonderful, they thought—like having your own petting zoo on your head!

But the girl's mother refused to pack the mice lunch or make them supper; so the girl had no choice but to share hers with them. Soon, the girl who wouldn't brush her hair found herself very hungry.

The girl also began to feel worried. Yes, she loved her companions. After all, they told funny knock-knock jokes and were very sweet to Baby. But they did not like the bath.

"We can't swim!" they chorused, clinging to knotted strands. "Don't do it! We'll drown!"

"That's silly," the girl said. "All mice can swim. We learned that in our unit on rodents."

"We'll overlook your name-calling," the mouse-king announced. He was the biggest one, who had arrived early on with the fairy-tale books in the suitcase. "But there will be NO BATHS. It's just our way." (They had learned this last part from listening to the girl.)

Much to the mice's relief, the girl agreed. For though she was becoming quite dirty, she had grown fond of their company. They had set up such a marvelous home for themselves—a palace, really, atop her head. It had secret passageways and a cheese cellar and a tiny circular moat.

But the not-bathing turned out to be less pleasing than the not-brushing had been. The girl was starting to . . . how shall we put this . . . she was starting to *smell*.

And so of course no one wanted to be near her. Even Baby tried to keep her distance! Now it was as if the mice were in charge of the girl, rather than the other way around.

The girl began to sleep less well. She was afraid, for
one thing, of smooshing the mice if she rolled over; and for
another, the mice were rather nocturnal, as it turned out.

They chattered all night, keeping up Baby, telling her complicated knock-knock jokes into the wee hours until the sun rose and the girl—bleary-eyed—climbed out of bed.

Each morning, after carefully brushing her teeth and dressing
(it was hard to pull a sweater over a head full of protesting mice),
she tidied up her mouse-palace head as best she could and dragged
herself, Baby, and all of the mice to school.

Then one terrible day, Teacher said, "I'm so sorry, but you can no longer bring Baby. Each child may have only *one friend* for naptime, and it appears that by now you have *one hundred mice* in your hair. The rules are quite broken enough!"

The girl slumped her shoulders and hung her heavy head as Baby and all of the mice stared at her in silence.

Oh, poor mice! Dear hairless Baby had been the girl's best friend since she herself had been hairless, and a baby. The girl needed Baby with her at school; that was that. "It's just my way," she wept.

$$\begin{array}{r} 2 \\ +2 \\ \hline 4 \end{array} \qquad \begin{array}{r} 1 \\ +3 \\ \hline 4 \end{array}$$

And so, that very night, the girl reluctantly bid the mice farewell. She had a calm talk with them first—explaining about the troubles with the not-washing, the not-taking hairless Baby to school, and the general, well, insomnia, really. And like all good mice, they understood.

Carefully, they packed their things and dismantled the palace.
Single-file, they took their leave, singing a mournful song:
  "O girl who would not brush her hair,
  Thank you for letting us live in there.
  We're on our way, our work is done.
  We'll find a new head to live upon."
(The mice were more clever with knock-knock jokes than with
songs, as it turned out; and, truth be told, they weren't very good at
knock-knock jokes.)

When the mice had all gone, the girl took a long, soapy bath with Baby perched on the edge of the tub. After that, she dressed herself and the doll in matching nightgowns with pictures of happy mice printed upon them. Sitting up in bed, she contentedly ran a brush through her shining mane. Then she kissed Baby, leaned back, closed her eyes, and began to dream.

In the morning, the other schoolchildren gathered around the girl. They marveled at her braids, and at the ingenious way she had tied a ribbon around Baby's hairless head. "It's just my way," the girl smiled.

Meanwhile, under the monkey bars, another girl, who lived next door to the girl who wouldn't brush her hair, was deep in argument with a couple of mice dangling from the ends of her wild pigtails.

Silly mice! That's just their way.